Original concept by

DISCARDED

Roger Hargreaves

Written and illustrated by

Adam Hargreaves

One day Mr Nonsense was reading the Nonsenseland Times when he had the idea of going to the moon.

"Well, if a cow can jump over it then it can't be too hard to get to," he announced to no one in particular.

Later that day he mentioned the idea to Mr Greedy.

Mr Greedy thought it was an excellent plan.

"I hear the moon's made of cheese," he said, licking his lips. "I like cheese."

But Mr Greedy did put Mr Nonsense straight about one thing.

"It's a very long, long way away."

So they went to see Mr Clever.

"What we need is a space rocket," explained Mr Clever. "A space rocket is something I've always wanted to build."

"Will that be very difficult?" asked Mr Nonsense.

"Well, it is rocket science, so the answer is yes," said Mr Clever, who rather likes to show off.

While Mr Clever built the rocket, the other two set about choosing fellow astronauts to travel with them.

Mr Nosey could not go because the space helmet would not fit over his nose.

Mr Tickle and Mr Tall could not go because neither of them could fit into the spacesuits!

And Little Miss Splendid refused to take off her hat which was no good at all.

Mr Clever had finished the rocket in record time, clever him, and the day of the launch arrived.

"Ten, nine, eight, seven, six, five, four, three, two, one, blast off!" cried Mr Clever, pressing the launch button.

But nothing happened.

Nothing happened because Mr Forgetful had forgotten to fill the fuel tank.

An hour later, the rocket took off, roaring up into the sky trailing a great cloud of smoke.

It rose higher and higher into the air, high above the earth, through the atmosphere and into outer space.

"Oh my!" cried Mr Worry. "I'm floating!"

And so he was.

And so was everyone else.

"We don't weigh so much in space," explained
Mr Clever, cleverly. "The air is much thinner up here."

"Unlike Mr Greedy," chipped in Mr Rude, rudely.

It wasn't long before Mr Greedy began to feel hungry, so he cooked spaghetti for everyone.

Perhaps not the most sensible idea!

When they arrived, Mr Nonsense was the first to walk on the moon because it had all been his idea.

Although, he kept an eye out for jumping cows.

It was Mr Worry who discovered strange footprints on the surface of the moon, which he followed; while worrying he was about to bump into a space alien.

He was rather relieved to find it was Little Miss Scary walking on her hands.

Mr Small could not believe it.

He could lift Mr Greedy above his head with one finger!

Everyone had a wonderful day on the moon.

Everyone except for Mr Greedy, who was disappointed to discover that the moon is not made of cheese.

"I told you so," said Mr Clever, something that Mr Clever never tires of saying.

The next day they packed up and went home.

It had been a splendid adventure and Mr Nonsense was very pleased with himself.

And so were all who lived in Nonsenseland.

All except one.

"Go to the moon? What nonsense."

Said the cow!